ONE MILE

HOW THE POWER OF

PRAYER SAVED ME

By: Gwendolyn Singleterry

ONE MILE:

HOW THE POWER OF PRAYER SVED ME

ISBN 978-1-940831-56-5

Copyright © 2019 by Gwendolyn Singleterry

Published by Mocy Publishing, LLC.

Website: www.mocypublishing.com

Email: info@mocypublishing.com

Phone: (833) 736-5483

TABLE OF CONTENTS

DEDICATION

HONOR FOR GWENDOLYN SINGLETERRY

FORWARD

DEDICATION

I dedicate this book to my daughter, Jonique Rance. There is no question that you have my heart forever.

To my sister, Bernice Ellis, I love you.

To my deceased mother, Annie McKibbens, and my brother Thurman T. Meirritts; whom I miss very much.

I dedicate this book to my brother's children: Miss. Chaonico Meirritts, Mrs. Bendolyn Smith and Mr. Derrick Merritts.

HONOR FOR GWENDOLYN SINGLETERRY

I have known Mother Gwen since 2011. I can't remember actually how we first connected, but I thank God every day that we did. I do remember seeing her at the Alter every Sunday worshiping with her tambourine in hand giving the Lord the highest praise. You could truly see the glory all over her. I remember thinking when I grow up that's how I want to be. She walked and dressed with authority and excellence, as if she know who her daddy (the Lord) was.

I remember sitting with her on Sunday and we begin talking about how good God was and all the wonderful things He has done in both our lives; before you know it we were both shouting and praising God. Mother Gwen is a true prayer warrior, when she said she was going to pray for you she meant it and you knew everything was going to be alight.

I remember when we were looking for mothers of the church for a Mother's Day video and the Lord told me to get

Mother Gwen. She is a mother to many not just I this church but for all the many people she has come in contact with. Mother Gwen has spoken in to my life many times when I would be at my lowest her words were always true and on time. She is truly a blessing to my family spiritually and naturally. When my mother passed away, she was right there holding me up in prayer and encouraging me to hold on and be strong. She was a blessing to my family during that rough time.

Not only is Mother Gwen a strong prayer warrior she is an awesome cook. When I say she can cook, she makes the best cakes and pies and that is putting it mildly. The best part about that is she prays about what kind of dessert she should make. My husband would always say thank God for Mother Gwen because she always hears from God. She does nothing without true direction form God and we love her so.

When Mother Gwen wrote her 1ˢᵗ book I was so blessed by it. It was the simple truth of her life with God. It gave me direction on how to walk and listen more closely to His voice; the one thing that has blessed me was to see Mother Gwenn never let the enemy keep her down. She always comes back with more power, greatness and stronger ready to serve God at the higher level. With her last setback due to her accident Mother Gwen was determined not to let the enemy keep her down, as always, her test now a greater testimony. I do believe that she is stronger and on fire for the Lord more today than ever before.

If there is one word to describe this true woman of God it would be "Anointed". The scripture that comes to mind for her would be Proverbs 31:30 I truly love her with all my heart and blessed to be one of her angels. I praise God to have this mighty, godly woman in my life. She truly one of my spiritual mothers   *~Cynthia A. Sweeting*

I met Gwen Singleterry 20 years ago when she was the sole proprietor of her cosmetology business and catering service. She is a talented and gifted cosmetologist, as well as an awesome cook. Her knowledge of proper hair care techniques produced hair growth and quality and fantastic styles. So much so that her customers shared their level of satisfaction with others which caused clients to come from miles away of all ages to her salon.

Gwen has a strong belief in God and an extensive knowledge of the bible. This knowledge has led her to minister to her clients while providing services to their hair. Consequently, this created an atmosphere of trust and love. As a result, Gwen was able to give advice to her clients who were in need to hear God's word. As of today, she is still providing God's word to her customers.

Gwen's catering service was very successful as well as her cosmetology business. For example, people from near and far came to order her delicious home cooked meals and exquisite desserts. That's because she added that down home country flavor from Georgia to each meal.

Still today, Gwen would prepare desserts for special occasions for her church. She also bakes cakes for customers of the beauty salon for their birthday, surprise them and their faces would light up.

To sum it up, Gwen is a stylist black woman from the past to the present. When she enters a room such as a church event, concert or dinner; people stop to admire her outfits, hats, how well coordinated the colors are and are amazed by how beautiful she looks.

Gwen has been known to share her fashion abilities with young people as it relates on how to dress and present themselves as God's child. She is not one to bite her tongue on giving advice.

She is a symbol of a strong black women. When the going gets rough, she knows who her provider is – GOD. She prays and have faith until she sees that breakthrough for that situation. She is not selfish with her prayers; she prays for all who needs prayer and counseling from the word of God.

~Marilyn Harris Puryear

FORWARD

There were nearly 40 years between us, yet our interaction was more like close high school girlfriends with much in common. We both had passion for original fashion, creating beauty in others, writing, intercession and mad love for all things Jesus. Usually all my visits were unannounced. Often met with praise/worship music or a powerful sermon streaming from under her door. I came to the rehabilitation center armed with a fresh CD from church, a Bible, a new journal... anything I believe she needed to simply know that she was not alone in her recovery.

The accident had broken bones, however, Sis. Singletary's spirit was stronger than ever. She was steady under the onslaught of this physical attack because she knew God and what He was saying was the final authority in her life. The Word says, "The effectual fervent prayer of the righteous avails much" (James 5:16b). An environment was created by her prayers that transcended her present situation. Every physical goal that her attendees and physical therapists gave her were exceeded before the time because Jesus walked in and divinely strengthened her capacity. She simply believed God.

It is no exaggeration that our hearts became knitted together during this process. Despite the painful journey, she chose to focus on Him and seize the opportunity to minister with precision to anyone that crossed her path. Always a consistent source of encouragement and just seemed to know things that were on my mind. We both were sensitive to pray for one another and it was no question that heaven was at work on her behalf.

Pull up a seat and witness first-hand God's healing power through the life of Sis. Gwendolyn Singletary. Just as I was extraordinarily blessed to have powerful visitations... I invite you to have the same experience as you flip through every page of her testimony.

I celebrate and love you.

~Shavon L. Stanley

THE ACCIDENT

January 13, 2018 wow God this is my anniversary month of moving to Michigan and it's been 60 years of me doing hair and I can hardly wait to retire. Well here we go God, help me get out of this bed and have a pain free day so I can take care of these 6 customers. The day ended like most of my days, yep, just another ordinary day – getting off work at 3:30 p.m. Just as I was about to leave one of my spiritual daughters called and we laughed as usual then said good bye. Now the question is do I go to the grocery story? I should, it's just a hop, skip and jump away. But it is so Icey out here. Yes, I might as well because it will be one less thing I have to do tomorrow. I pulled out of the salon parking lot and drove east on 11 mile road, then turned north on Lasher, then turned east onto 12 Mile Road. As everyone knows at 79.5

years old and driving in winter conditions, I am a very slow driver.

But out of nowhere a force picked the car up and put it over the curb and landed on the grass of a school in front of the school's sign. The car stopped, the motor was turned off, it just sat there. I asked God what is wrong with this car. Then, suddenly, the car began to levitate, I saw a big black tree and I began to scream, "Jesus" and I passed out. When I regained some level of consciousness, I realized the car hit the brick wall of a fire station at Evergreen Road and 12 Mile Road; located 1 mile from the school. I opened my eyes and I heard firemen talking and trying to get me out of the car. In the distance I saw a man on the phone, while EMS was trying to put me on the gurney. One thing I will never forget is the excruciating pain I experienced by the impact of my body being crumpled inside of the car.

I was taken to Beaumont hospital still in and out of consciousness, but I do remember there were a ton of medical people touching and all talking to me at the same time. I heard a familiar voice and it was the spiritual daughter I spoke with just before leaving the salon – she was calling my name. The doctors told me I was in serious condition, they needed to cut my clothes off me because I was covered in glass and needed to get me stabilized. I was in intensive care for 2 days before they moved me to a regular room. The doctors told me I had punctured lungs, fractured ribs and cut the kidney.

During the 1st week in the hospital Brother and Sister James from my church came to visit, they prayed over me and gave me a prayer cloth. I was so happy to receive the prayer cloth because I understand the power and purpose of the cloth. Prayer cloths are mentioned in the bible in Acts 19:11-12

(Amplified Bible – Joyce Meyer Version), "And God did unusual and extraordinary miracles by the hands of Paul, so that handkerchiefs or towels or aprons which had touched his skin were carried away and put upon the sick, and their diseases left them and the evil sprites came out to them"

It is nothing for God to do His good works suddenly. So much so that the next day after placing the prayer cloth over my body I rang for the nurse to come and assist me sitting up in the bed so I can prepare myself mentally for the pain of turning my body to get out of the bed to go to the rest room. Well, the nurse in my opinion took too long so I decided to walk by faith and not by sight. And look at God – I was able to sit up in the bed and placed my legs to the side of the bed. By the time the nurse arrived to assist me and saw me sitting up she was shocked. I told the nurse this is not of my own doing, this is the strength of God. And for the remaining days in the hospital God gave me the strength to set up without the nurse assisting me. Praise His holy name!

Within 2 weeks the doctor told me I was being released and could now begin rehab.

REHAB

I was moved from Beaumont hospital to Maple Manor Rehab in Novi, Michigan. My therapist asked what my goal was. I told him my goal is to be walking by my birthday April 5th, which was 9 weeks and 3 days away. My reason was I would be 80 years old and I did not want to look like what I had been through. I'm was not interested in hoping along for the rest of my life.

Still in rehab, talking to God, I told Him I can take myself to the bathroom and walk around my room without any body helping me and just use the walker. Later my therapist came, and we walked to the therapy room as I used the walker. After our session she told me I was getting promoted because I'd progressed to the point where I can now take myself to the bathroom and walk around the bedroom with only the walker and no one helping me. I told her she must have heard from God because that is what I prayed for. After our conversation the hospital upgraded me to "independent person in room". I called it "the walker" instead of "my walker" because I did not want any ownership in depending on a device to help me walk.

Friends (2 married couples) from my church came to visit and we had an awesome time laughing, talking and praying. One of the brothers told how the Lord called him and his wife into the ministry to pray for the sick. His wife stated recently she had a dream that she and her husband were praying for a sick person, but she did not see their face. But when they were told about me being in an accident the Holy Spirit revealed to them that I was the person in the dream. Before leaving they gave me and the other couple a prayer cloth. The other couple stayed a while longer and we continued to fellowship. While we were fellowshipping, the wife stopped talking and said, "Ms Gwen, do you see what you just did?" I said, No. She told me I had crossed my legs and at that time a glow appeared around my body. I looked down and my, my, my, she was right, my legs were crossed. God's healing power allowed me to cross my legs pain free till I hadn't noticed until she brought it to my attention. I asked her to take a picture of me and send it to my daughter so she could see the progress I'd made and tell it to the other couple when they see each other in church.

Another friend that I attend the River church with provided me a CD of the January 14, 2018, message by Pastor Tim Walker who was a guest speaker. Pastor Walker taught on the scripture regarding the women that bled for 12 years and how she was healed by touching the hem of Jesus' garment. When I received the CD, God told me to play it every night when I go to bed and listen to it using my ear plugs. As I continued to play the cd each time, I felt healing taking place in my body. My pastor also gave me a CD named "Stirring the Waters of The Supernatural". My soul was blessed. I worshipped, prayed in tongues and praised God. It was afterwards that God told me to play this CD first thing every morning.

I was talking to God about me walking without the walker in my room. My therapist said, you can walk without your walker in your room. I told her that she had heard from God. That night I cleaned myself, put my night gown on by myself. That night I needed to go to the bathroom I was getting ready to ring the bell for the nurse. The Lord told me I didn't need any help. He was there. I got myself up and put myself into the bed without the nurses' help.

I had an encounter with God. This angel was standing in front of me and began to work on my left side with my fractured ribs. I said Lord how he knows did you tell him God. One of my church members came to visit on her way to service and we began to praise God. Around 12:00 that day God remined me that I had not had a pain pill since Saturday.

Normally I would have taken pain pill 2-3 times that day. With tears in my eyes my body was free from pain and I gave God the praise.

With one more week left before being released from rehab a series of tests were given and I was told by medical staff that I'd passed the tests. The next day I went to therapy, came back about 11:15 a.m. waiting for lunch and the medical team came to my room to do a chest x-ray and left to have them developed. Within 15 minutes the team rushed back into my room with a doctor asking questions about my breathing all while telling me that my lung is collapsing and rushed me to Providence Hospital in Novi, Michigan. They performed surgery immediately. This was the 2nd operation on my lungs. I was released 7 days later. One week after being released I went back for my checkup and the doctor announced that my lung was completely healed. Praise God, in Jesus name. I give all praise to my Father. He put me back together in 8 weeks. God is so good that He gave me the desire of my heart which was to be home and walking by my birthday. But not only did He do that for me, He also allowed my family to come from out of town including my daughter and local friends to be present and we celebrated my birthday. Psalm 37:4 KJV, "Delight thyself also in the Lord and He shall give the desires of thine heart."   God in many ways speak to us. Declaring his wealth and our improvement. I am the maker of all things the wealth and glory are mine.

RETURNING BACK TO WORK

I got to church early, music was playing, I went to the alter I began to walk and pray. I did my praise dance. God and I had a good time. I asked God to turn the bible class into a Holy Ghost Sunday evening service. I asked Him to use the man of God. He did just that. The Pastor stated that God had sent an angel in the service for people looking for jobs. Pastor asked whomever is here believing for a better job, come forward for prayer. The Holy Ghost wrecked the service and job was in the atmosphere. And guess what – I received a job.

Within the same month God opened the door for me to go back to work for a season. The Lord said, go shopping and take your supplies to the salon now. So, I was obedient to God and went shopping for supplies. I wanted everything to be in place by Friday. I called my neighbor and asked if she would take me to the salon and she said yes but had some business to take care of first. She stated she would call me when she got home. I was relaxing on the sofa reading while waiting for her to get back with me. About 2:00 p.m. the Lord spoke to me. He said, you have a roller cart someone gave you that has never been used. Get up and see if your supplies will fit. God reminded me that it was the cart I blessed my sister with for her to take when grocery shopping, and it appeared to give her supernatural strength. God said it will do the same for me. I got up and got the rolling cart, put my supplies inside and it fit perfectly. I have 2 plastic containers, and God told me to put them in a plastic bag, and not take my purse, but take my keys and phone.

I walked to work most days. It was an awesome walk not too hot and an awesome breeze, as if God was standing behind me pushing me along the way. I couldn't believe how fast I walked to the salon. My coworkers asked me how I got to work. I told them I walked. They were shocked.

Just as I put everything in its place, in walked a costumer and they asked if I would perm and cut her hair. I said yes. I started working on the customer when another customer walked in. This customer wanted color and a trim; they asked me to take her too. While working on the customer my telephone rang and it was my neighbor wanting to know if I wanted a ride to the salon, I told her I was already at the salon. She was surprised and asked me to call her when I want to go home. I have learned when God speaks you need to obey them. God new he was sending those two ladies and He did not want me to miss my blessing.

A WALK TO THE POST OFFICE

I ordered a package, when it came, I wasn't home, so the delivery person took it back to the post office. I was thinking, who could I call to take me to the post office, but I couldn't think of anyone. So, I laid on the sofa and started reading. The Lord spoke to me and He said, get up and walk to the post office. He said, I got you. I got there so fast and I said to the Lord, how did you get me here so fast. I was not tired. The walk was about 15 to 20 minutes. I got the package and walked back home and we not tired when I made it home. I don't worry about how I feel because I know God got me.

THE POWER OF PRAYER

Get you a war room so you can have a inner line of communication between you and your God. Your life will be transformed and blessed. People who pray are people that have been inspired, strong, courageous, happy, successful and confident. Prayer will heal you, prosper you and bring you into joy as you have never known. Pray now and see what prayer can do for you.

Prayer is mighty in its operation, and God never disappoints those who put their trust and confidence in Him.   Praying give sense, brings wisdom, broaden and strengthen the mind. Prayer opens an outlet for the promise, removes the hindrances in the way of their execution, puts them into working order, and secures their glorious end. It's success and power depend on man's ability to pray. I do not believe there is any problems, any defeat, any difficulty that cannot be overcome through prayer.

What is critically important to know about the power of prayer is to pray for things that align with the will of God. Meaning do not pray for things that fall under the title of sin. For example, praying that a man leaves his wife to marry you; praying that harm comes to someone; praying that harm comes to an ethnic group. Also do not use prayer like a gift card, thinking God is a genie. Pray for those things that prosper and heal or protect others or yourself and family. Mark 11:22-26 Amplified (Joyce Meyer Version), "And Jesus, replying, said to them, have faith in God constantly; Truly I tell you, whoever says to this mountain, Be lifted up and thrown into the sea! And does not doubt at all in his heart but believers that what eh says will take place, it will be done for him, for this reason I am telling you, whatever you ask for in prayer, believe trust and be confident that is granted to you, and you will get it. An whenever you stand praying, if you have anything against anyone, forgive him and let it drop, leave it, let it go, in order that your Father, Who is in haven may also forgive you your own failings and shortcomings and let them drop. But if you do not forgive, neither will your Father in heaven forgive your failings and shortcomings."

Also don't be afraid to pray for pray for healing, wisdom or favor over your life and for others:

Luke 5:12 – 13 Amplified (Joyce Meyer Version), "While He was in one of the towns, there came a man full of covered with leprosy; and when he saw Jesus, he fell on his face and implored Him, saying, Lord, if You are willing, you are able to cure me and make me clean. And Jesus reached out his hand and touched him, saying, I am willing; be cleansed! And immediately the leprosy left him." Psalms 147:3 Amplified (Joyce Meyer Version), "He heals the brokenhearted and binds up their wounds, curing their pains and their sorrows."

Amplified (Joyce Meyer Version): James 1:5, "If any of you is deficient in wisdom, let him ask of "the giving God" who gives to everyone liberally and ungrudgingly, without reproaching or faultfinding, and it will be given to him."

Deuteronomy 28 1-14 Amplified (Joyce Meyer Version), "If you will listen diligently to the voice of the Lord your God, being watchful to do all His commandments which I command you this day, the Lord your God will set you high above al the nations of the earth, And all this blessings shall come upon you and overtake you if you heed the voice of the Lord your God."

When you pray have the mind of a pit bull. "There is no physical locking mechanism in the jaws of a pit bull, their jaw physiology is no different from any other breed. What is different about pit bulls is their psychology, which is why you cannot train even the most biddable dogs like border collies or the easy peasy lab to hang on a rope. **The jaws of a pit bull** do not technically lock but pit bulls often grab hold of their

target and refuse to let go".

When we clamp down on the truth and promise of God's word we should not let go until it manifests itself in our life. Nobody or nothing should shake us loose because we are covered by God's word which has the final say. God is not a liar. Jeremiah 1:12 KJV, "Then said the Lord onto me thou have well seen for I will hasten my word to perform it"; Deuteronomy 28 1-14 Amplified (Joyce Meyer Version): Then said the Lord to me, You have seen well for I am alert and active, watching over My word to perform it.

THE SENSE OF GOD'S PRESENCE

As we obey the leading of the Spirit of God, we enable God to answer the prayer of other people. I mean that our lives, my life, is the answer to someone's prayer, perhaps from centuries ago. I have the unspeakable knowledge that my life is the answer to prayers and that God is blessing me and making me a blessing entirely of his sovereign grace and nothing to do with my merits, except as I am bold enough to trust his leading and not the dictates of my own wisdom and common sense. The sense of "my Father" has been wonderful.

ANGEL, ANGEL, ANGEL

I went to my bedroom, got on the bed to read and pray. I had a visitation of an Angel. He told me what he was going to do for me. I heard his voice very clear. When I came to, I was in a state of shock. Just as I opened my eyes, I saw a flicker of white movements and I knew that the Angel was leaving me. I was in a state of shock from what I experienced.

I prayed, cried and worshipped God. I gave God all the glory. Psalm 95:6 KJV, "O' come let us worship and bow down let us kneel before the Lord our maker."

THE GREATER REVELATION

To know who you are in Christ Jesus – you are a Priest. First Peter 2:9 KJV, "But ye are a chosen generation, a peculiar people, that ye should share the praised of Hi who hath faith called you out of darkness into marvelous light. For such a high priest became us. Who is holy, harmless, undefiled, separate from sinners and made higher than the heavens. We are to declare His works. We are to live a holy life because we represent Christ our Savior. We are to walk like Jesus and live a holy life that we may be fisherman of men. Jesus we can do greater works. There is a sense in which every Christian may properly be called priest.

First Peter 2:5 KJV, "Ye also as …stones, are priesthood, to offer up spiritual sacrifices, acceptable to God by Jesus Christ."

Revelation 1:6 KJV, "And hath made us kings and priest unto God and his father to him be glory and dominion for ever and ever amen."

MOVING FORWARD

God has given us dominion. When we stay in God's word we will have power to overcome anything that the devil sends your way. He had given us the power to overcome everything if we stay connected to Him through his word and prayer. You are free by God's grace. Sin is no longer your master, for you are no longer subject to the law, which enslave you to sing. Instead you are free by God's grace. God will establish your steps and direct them by His Words. Psalms 145:13 KJV, "Thy kingdom is an everlasting kingdom, and thy dominion endure throughout all generations."

Second Cor 1:24 KJV, "Not for that we have dominion over your faith but are helpers of your joy; for my faith ye stand".

First Peter 4:11 KJV, "If any man speaks let him speak as the oracle of God; if any man minister, let him do it as of the ability which God giveth that God in are things may be glorified through Jesus Christ giveth, that God in all things may be glorified through Jesus Christ, to whom be praised

and dominion forever and ever.

Because of the wondrous work on the cross; The marvelous price he paid which included a sashing of sometimes beyond our imagination and an acquittal releasing the entire human race from a place of sin to one of righteousness. From a debt to Satan as (He made an open show of that ole devil) has made us righteous, so we can come boldly to the throne of grace to obtain help and glory to God that grace which is strength through all the throws and issues of living life.

We come unashamed and unafraid. Each day new mercy laced with favor we yield to Him and allow His life changing Word to do just that! Every chain must break! Every ill of life must surrender to the power of his redeeming love. So, we come and we are confident that He hears us because we release every care and forgive others as H so lovingly forgave us. Armed with His Word defying every threat. The care that someone wronged us or tried to destroy us.

All the secrets, lies, disappointments, sickness and diseases that try to bind us and hinder us from fulfilling His will in us.

Whether they be human or supernatural. He is our authority! We believe Him in our hearts and agree with Him with our mouths with His powerful Word that has the ability to find those places in our lives where human hands cannot heal right down between the marrow and the bone. We emerge with the victory in His wonderful and matchless Name!

The only Name given whereby we must be saved. The sweetest Name I know.

Sweet hour of prayer that leads me from a world of care. Make all my needs and wishes known. In seasons of distress and grief my soul has often found relief. And often escaped

the tempters snare by thy return sweet hour of prayer.

By Him for Him.

www.ingramcontent.com/pod-product-compliance
Lightning Source LLC
Chambersburg PA
CBHW041030170626
46815CB00001B/30